Give your child a head start with
PICTURE READERS

Dear Parent,

Now children as young as preschool age can have the fun and satisfaction of reading a book all on their own.

In every Picture Reader, there are simple words, rebus pictures, and 24 flash cards to cut out and keep. (There is a flash card for every rebus picture plus extra cards for reading practice.) After children listen to each story a couple of times, they will be ready to try it all by themselves.

Collect all the titles in our Picture Reader series. Once children have mastered these books, they can move on to Levels 1, 2, and 3 in our All Aboard Reading series.

To Megan at three—
Love,
Mom and Dad

ISBN 0-448-41295-0   G H I J

ALL ABOARD READING™

A PICTURE READER

PICKY NICKY

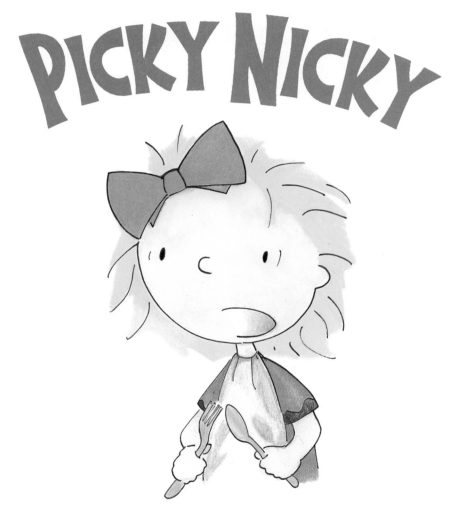

**By Cathy East Dubowski and
Mark Dubowski**

Grosset & Dunlap • New York

Mom and Dad say,

"Supper is ready!"

Picky Nicky says,

"I want !"

Mom says, "No 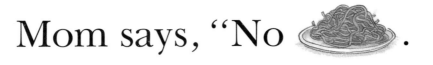 .

We are having

and  ."

Picky Nicky says,

"I would rather eat

 and

than and !"

Dad says,

"We are also having

 and .""

Picky Nicky says,

"I would rather eat

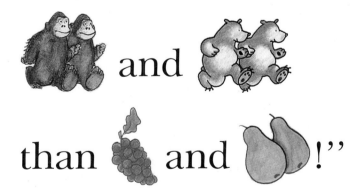 and

than and !""

Picky Nicky says,

"Freddy always

has  !"

Dad says,

"Then go eat

at Freddy's  !"

So Picky Nicky

goes to Freddy's .

She goes to the .

She rings the .

"What's for supper?"

she says.

"It's !" says Freddy.

"Get a !"

Freddy's mom

brings the .

Then she says,

"We are also having ,

, , and .

Pass your !"

Oh, no!

Picky Nicky thinks,

"I would rather eat

, and   ,

than   ,   ,

, and   !"

What will she do?

"I know!"

Picky Nicky takes

a  of ,

a of ,

some , and

a little bit of .

She hides them

under her !

Soon her 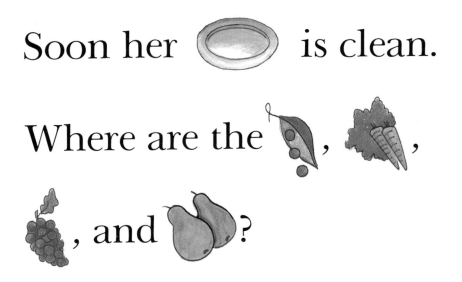 is clean.

Where are the 🫛, 🥕,

🍇, and 🍐?

Wow!

Picky Nicky ate them!

The next night

Picky Nicky says,

"I will eat anything—

if I can hide it

in ."

Dad says, "Even ,

, , and ?

Even ?"

Picky Nicky says,

"No, I will have

my

all by itself!"

peas	spaghetti
bee	carrot
grapes	parrot

ape	pear
house	bear
bell	door

spoon	plate
table	ice cream
star	bus

truck	sun
book	bike
bed	apple